JUNE 25

On the Road to You

Shally Gulshan Sharma

Invincible Publishers

First published in India in 2018

ISBN: 978-93-87328-53-2

Invincible Publishers
G-120, Sushant Lok III, Sector 57, Gurgaon-122002

Registered Address: Opposite Kasturba Ashram,
Radaur, Haryana - 135133

Printed at Thomson Press (India) LTD

I dedicate this book entirely to my love, my husband

Gulshan Sharma

whose eternal love and support for me breathes LIFE into me!

Acknowledgement

A book is not just a mere collection of chapters; it is rather a collection of some unheard experiences, voices and unexpressed feelings. With this book, I have just started my journey as an author. I had been planning to pen down this story for the last couple of years and now it has finally come to be.

My husband Gulshan Sharma has always encouraged and supported me for everything I ever wanted to do or achieve. He believes in me and my capabilities more than my own self. Whatever I am today, is only because of his eternal love and support towards me. He is my entire universe, my love and my everything. If I have been able to complete this book, it's only because of him. I also thank Mr. Sanjay Chauhan, Mr. Jasmer Singh Godia and all Gulshan's friends, for standing with us always!

I thank my Badi Maa (Smt. Pushpa Sharma) and Choti Maa (Smt. Indu Bala Sharma) for their constant motivation and support towards me. Your guidance and motivation keeps us moving ahead in life.
I express my sincere gratitude to the entire team of Invincible Publishers for their dedicated effort in the making of this book, and my editor, Aditi Saxena, for her valuable inputs and suggestions.

This book is not just a story, but a journey!

4 years ago…

No matter where you've come from,
No matter where you've been.

There will always be some part of you,
Which will always remain unseen.

So, open your eyes wide enough to catch that unseen sight,
'Cause you live only once and you better do that right!

CHAPTER ONE

14th December 2013, 06:10 P.M.

"A bit more, just for five more minutes and I'll get it. Exactly, it's going perfect," I say to myself in low whispers.

I can feel the movement of my leg muscles, the pain reaching down to my calves and my heart pounding faster than normal. My sight blacks out, recalling all those times when I have been rejected, when my freedom to go for my own choices got rejected.

I can't let it happen all the time. This rejection is killing me.

I then press the stop button on the treadmill, regaining my normal breathing pattern. I go to sit at the staircase near the gym's reception and look at my face in the long, wall-like mirrors all around me. The sweat drops on my face twinkle, as if to say that it's enough for the day. There are sweat patches on my T-shirt. Drenched hair fall over my forehead and irritate me. Keeping my hands crossed over my knees, I start looking at the floor, lost deep in thoughts. Suddenly, I hear a voice saying, "Come on! Come on, girl! Not more than ten minutes of rest. Get up."

It's my gym trainer, Alex. He has been in this profession for the last twelve years. With a perfect sculpted body, he doesn't look any less than a knight. Every time I look at him, I can clearly see every movement of his muscle, whether it is when he talks to me, when he picks up a dumbbell, or even when he trains the other guys at the gym.

It's only been a week since I pushed myself into a gym. Before this, I hadn't ever thought of working on my body. I hardly have any knowledge of the exercises that people do here, or of the heavy machines on which they sweat. But thanks to Alex and his help, I have now begun to get a grasp of these things.

"Stop day dreaming, girl! Either you start working hard or just go home," he says to me in a loud tone.

I have no option left but to get up and continue with my exercises.

With a few more sets of tedious exercises, I look at myself in the mirror, trying to figure out how much rounder my hips have grown or how cool my abs look. Unfortunately, it's all only in my mind at the moment, but I am happy still.

"It's already 8:59 P.M. Mom might call me up any moment now," I remind myself.

I hurry up, put my not-so-funky green colored jacket back on and start toddling towards home.

It's not very far, but it gives me a good fifteen minutes' walk after the gym.

"I don't want to go back home now. Why can't I workout the whole day and then the entire night? Nobody besides me with those heavy machines around me. Mirrors all over the walls, being the only source of distraction. I just keep looking at myself, and at every part of my entire body, how it moves when I am on the treadmill. The curves! It feels so good to be lost in yourself, isn't it?" my mind starts talking again.

On my way home, hundreds of thoughts strike my mind.

Suddenly, in between my small and steady steps, I accidentally trip over a piece of rock. When I gaze around, I see so many pairs of eyes on me. Those unfamiliar eyes, constantly staring at you, checking you out from top to bottom, the ones that look at you as if you are an alien. There are people passing by, carrying different smells, some talking on phone and discussing their late night plans, fruit vendors hawking their day's stock, guys on bikes making weird sounds while passing me by. I pace up my steps and finally reach home.

Home-sweet-home!

Don't judge me with your materialistic eyes,
Don't tell me, to follow all those lies.

'Cause, I'm a free spirit with a vision to fly high,
And I have less time to captivate my joys.

I'm telling you,
I'm telling you to not cross my ways,
As you'll regret it later in your days…

CHAPTER TWO

14th December 2013, 9:20 P.M.

My house is a bungalow-like set up near a very busy street, with a big maroon-colored gate which is carved with antique figures in gold paint. It makes a screeching sound every time it is being closed or opened. I live here, or rather on the first floor of it, with my family.

I open the gate carefully, trying to avoid the irritating noise it makes everytime, but it doesn't work out. With thousands of thoughts crossing my mind, I walk upstairs towards my room, which opens right beside the main entrance of the house.

"Sarah! where have you been? Do you even realize what time it is?" my mother shouts at me, when I am just about to take off my sports shoes.

"I'll have to complain about this to your father now. You have slipped out of my hands. I can't tolerate this anymore. I don't understand what the need is of joining a gym? You are just wasting our money. Working out at the gym won't make you look good, you'll stay the same old dark-skinned girl. I know the mentality of girls these days.

You just wait! Let me speak to your father tonight itself!" she continues and then walks back into her room in rage.

"Things will turn out good for me!" I keep repeating this to convince myself that I am more than just a dark skinned girl.

It's nothing new for me. I have always been taught to stay with the same old conservative mentality. To not go out, to speak in a low tone, to do only what I am asked to do, to never argue with anyone, to agree with everyone's opinion, and most importantly, to remember that the parents are always right, so there is no point of having a discussion with them; these are the guidelines that I have grown up with. For my parents, I am nothing more than an unwanted responsibility. They've never trusted me, neither did they ever trust my dreams. I still remember, once when I was in second standard, I used to watch all my classmates play in the playground together from my balcony and think, "Why can't I go and join my friends? Why don't I have the liberty to just play with my friends?" I don't think that was too big a demand for my parents to grant.

My mother never allowed me to visit any of my friends, not even if it was a girl. I was so isolated from the world around me that I hardly remember anything happy about my childhood. Sometimes, I used to get so frustrated that I would start talking to my own shadow. It's hard to describe the feelings of an eleven year old complaining about solitude. It gets even worse when there is no one to complain to, except your own shadow.

I unlace my shoes and walk towards my room. This room serves the purpose of both a store and a study room. There is no place to sleep, actually, just a single chair to accommodate oneself in and medium sized table. I have pasted many posters here with quotes on them. There is a heap of books on the study table, a pen-stand which I decorated using some old newspapers and some old artificial flowers in a vase placed on the upper shelf, a ceiling fan and some old scrap lying in one corner of the room.

Still, I love this place a lot. It is much better than a king sized room for me. I can spend my entire day here because this room belongs entirely to me. It listens to my voice, my thoughts, my joy and my sorrows. It lets me believe in myself and gives me so much peace that I forget all my worries. Here, I have no one to answer to, it's just me and my room.

I then change my clothes and rush to the kitchen to have a lemonade.

Take a break,

Take a break and look around.

Question yourself,

Question yourself about your mental ground.

Make sure, you are well versed with the syllabus of your life,

'Cause, there is no way back once you thrive.

CHAPTER THREE

15th December 2013, 8:50 A.M.

"Oh God! I am already late. What do I wear to college today? Let's wear this tee. I'll manage to match it up with that blue jeans. Ya! That's fine," I keep mumbling to myself while getting ready for college.

"Sarah! Go get my shoes," my younger brother orders me while tucking his shirt.

He is in 9th standard now, but is very careless towards his studies. "Listen Danish, I am already late for college. You get your shoes yourself," I tell him.

"Mom! This girl is so busy putting on kajal that she can't even help me get my shoes. I mean, why don't you scold her? Her daily tantrums are getting harder to manage," my brother continues to shout and yell at me.

"Bye, Mom. Bye, Dad," I say and leave the house without extending the argument.

Rushing towards the bus-stop, I keep a check on my watch. Simultaneously, I call up Sam, my bus-mate, to ensure that the bus hasn't crossed my stop yet.

"Hey! Sam, has the bus passed my stop?" I ask Sam.

"No, no! Not yet. Don't worry, I'll take care that the driver doesn't miss your stop."

"Thanks, dear!"

Finally, my college bus reaches my stop and I manage to grab the front seat on it.

"Hey! Sarah, got late for the bus again?" my classmate Sam calls me from the back seats.

"Yes, Sam! I just couldn't wake up on time in the morning. I was working on the German assignment till quite late last night," I say.

"Thanks for doing it for me. Hahahahaha!"

"Ya, ya, my pleasure."

Sam is an easy-going, loving guy. His ever-smiling face is infectious. No matter how stressed out he might be with his college affairs, his girlfriends, his breakups, he always shows his brighter side to others. Girls in our batch are mad for his dimples, but it hardly fascinates me.

It takes almost forty five minutes to commute to my college via bus, but I love this journey. I like peeping out the window of the bus and watch those unknown faces go by. There are so many faces, each holding a purpose in their eyes. I see those corporate guys, each with a suitcase in their hands, walking steadily to grab a taxi; a lady, looking very sexy in her cropped dress, who makes me wonder whether she is into fashion designing; those travelling on their bikes, cars and bicycles; kids walking along the footpath; everyone is rushing for one thing or the other in this world.

We hardly have anytime to sit back and relax, and to interact with our inner soul. We don't even know what we are rushing after, or if it would really give us happiness, or if we are doing it just because of the pre-set protocol. Are we driven by our needs, or our passions, or is it entirely aimless? I mean, we are not machines, then why we are working like one?

Take pride in being yourself, 'cause not everybody can do it.

Take pride in praising yourself, as not everybody can afford it.

For this, you may need to pay a lot,

But never stop striving for your own self!

CHAPTER FOUR

15th December 2013, 10:00 A.M.

I have finally reached college. It is an amazing place to be at. It is situated on the outskirts of the city and has an amazing view of lush green trees, farms and an amazing climate. There's always a fresh breeze blowing here. I take a deep breath and feel the breeze dancing through my hair, and convince myself that it will be a beautiful day. I then rush for my first lecture at B block, on the fourth floor.

"May I come in, sir?" I ask the professor, almost breathless from my run.

"Hmm," he nods his head in an uninteresting manner.

"Saraaahhhhhh! You have come…" shouts Joe. Joe is my college friend and an amazing guy.

"Yup! Finally," I say.

Joe keeps me laughing all day with his stupid jokes and weird sense of sarcasm. We both share an amazing bond of togetherness.

After four continuous boring lectures of forty five minutes each, we finally rush to the college mess, which always turns into a flea market at lunch time. Somehow, we both manage to join the counter queue and order some Chilly Potato and Fried Rice with Manchurian. Grabbing the food, we then rush to find a good place to sit. Not being able to manage that, we find a corner to sit on the staircase which goes down to the college basement.

"So, what's up with you? Why so upset?" Joe asks me out of curiosity.

"Umm, what? Nothing. All good!" I lie.

"Speak it out, man! You can count on me," Joe insists.

"I am fed up with this…" I say after a long pause. "Since childhood, this has been happening to me. My own people, my family, they don't understand me. I feel captivated in my own self. I can't even follow my heart, I am not allowed to talk to anyone, not allowed to go out on my own, not allowed to do what I like. When will all this end?" I continue to say.

"Listen, don't worry. Things will be fine soon. I know some of my school friends who used to complain about the same thing you are going through now. After a while, their parents started understanding them," he assures me, wanting me to stay positive.

"Umm, okay!" I end the conversation.

"Hey, what's that?"

"What?"

"See, you have grown biceps. Haha!" he makes fun of me.

"Ya, ya, I have," I partake in his joke.

"You didn't tell me how your gym is going?" I know that he is looking for some entertainment related to the gym thing.

"It's only been a week, yaa. It's going good till now. Let's see," I say.

"Your parents allowed you for that?" he continues to ask.

"Haha, I had to starve for 3 days and save some 70% of the gym's fees from my own pocket money to convince my parents. A hell lot of argument was still had. Pheww! I can't explain it," I tell him.

"Cool, man. Your life is so full of drama. You must never get bored, ever," he continues to make fun of me.

"Hmm, I wish I could laugh at this too," I speak out softly to him.

We then rush for our remaining lectures of the day.

Life is uncertain and so is the fate of a flowing river.

So, free yourself and find peace,

Find peace for your inner soul.

CHAPTER FIVE

15th December 2013, 06:15 P.M.

I get all excited for the gym as evening arrives. I feel like I am in love with those machines. In those loose tracks and a medium sized tee, I hit the gym like a super bodybuilder. I push open the gym's glass door at the entrance in full swing and give the trainer a cunning smile.

There is a register at the reception in which every one needs to write their in-out timings everyday. This is just for the purpose of tracking attendance. Resting one hand on my waist, I open the register and start filling up my name and my in timing.

"Umm, I.D. No. 27. Name, Sarah and time…" I start mumbling while filling the details.

Suddenly, my pen stops. I feel as if someone is staring at me. I turn around and my eyes catch hold of a charming guy standing right beside me. His honey-brown eyes were gazing straight into mine and I feel as if my heart skipped a beat.

I pass a smile at him and he reciprocates just the same. Reminding myself why I am holding a pen in my hand, I quickly get back to the register and fill out my in-time.

"Sarah, if you are done with the entry, can we start warm-up?" Alex beckons to me in a loud tone.

"Yes, we can," I reply and give Alex a weird look.

I go to the locker room then to remove my jacket and deposit my gym bag. After some dynamic stretches, Alex makes me move my arms in big circles in both directions, kick my legs forward, try to touch my toes and then try to reach for the sky. He then asks me to run on the treadmill for about five to ten minutes.

Before continuing, I go to the water cooler at one far corner of the gym to have some good three to four glasses of water, as I was dying of thirst.

After gulping two full glasses of water, I fill up my third glass and sit on the abdominal crunch machine nearby. I turn my head slightly to the right and gaze at everyone working out on the gym floor. Some were doing push-ups, some were cycling, while some were on the machines. Suddenly, I notice something.

A guy is doing dumbbell overhead squats. I can't see his face, but I can see his body's posture from the back. It seems like he has a perfectly toned body. He is around six feet tall, I guess. He is wearing a tight fitted black vest and blue shorts. I can see his muscles flex as he bends down and rises again with those dumbbells. His body is not too brawny like that of a body builder, yet he seems like a perfect masterpiece of masculinity. Those pumping muscles seem to have been carved out on his body. His back is towards me. I bend forward a little to see his face and find out that it is the same guy whom I had smiled at.

He is still gazing at me through those wall-length mirrors. He is squatting with dumbbells in his hands and his mesmerizing eyes on me.

My eyes get locked with his again. I suddenly start feeling uncomfortable. I hastily gulp the water down and get back to the treadmill.

I try to finish off with my set of exercises without looking into the mirrors surrounding me. I feel this guy's presence all around me, and his intimidating gaze on my whole body. I don't want to look back into his eyes. After the last few sets of crunches, I go back home, taking with me some unknown feeling.

CHANGE will happen, never be afraid to accept it.

As it's the only constant.

Embrace it with open arms and a wide smile.

CHAPTER SIX

15th December 2013, 11:30 P.M.

After completing a college assignment and tucking the handwritten notes in a transparent stick folder with my name and enrolment details written over it, I find myself lost in thoughts. My pen stops as I scribe my name over that A4 sheet at the same instance as it had at the gym.

I pause for a while and lean back in my chair. While I stare at the ceiling, my mind drives me to the same place where I first saw that handsome guy at the gym. I recall everything about my day's visit to the gym. Everything is crystal clear as if it is happening right in front of me all over again. The white ceiling of my room suddenly turns into a projector and I see everything replaying over it; his gaze, his smile, the pumping of his muscles during workout, those calves and more than anything else, those intimidating eyes which I can never forget. It feels like he is still looking at me from somewhere. I close my eyes and bend my head down on the table. I still can't stop myself from thinking about him.

"Why the hell is my mind getting so restless?" I ask myself.

Suddenly, I feel my heart pounding faster than normal and my breathing gets hitched up. I take a deep breath and exhale the air forcefully through my mouth. I repeat this a couple of times to get my breathing back to normal.

Not able to control my thoughts anymore, I go to the kitchen and prepare a bowl of noodles for myself. I believe that food is the best way to bring one's mind back to its normal state from a disturbed one.

"Perfect! A bowl of spicy noodles with a cup of ginger tea," I feel happy at successfully distracting myself from those thoughts.

"Alex would kill me if he comes to know that I am not following my diet, but it's okay sometimes, I guess. Right?" I keep mumbling and smiling.

When it was only my first day at the gym, I had very specific thoughts on how I wanted myself to look in a few months. I had repeatedly told him that I wanted toned thighs, a good waistline, a slim figure and all that.

He had laughing at me that time. All he said finally was that it all depended on how much I worked out, how much effort I put into myself and that it's not just about losing the weight, but about giving yourself a new identity, molding yourself into a new YOU.

Sometimes it's good to

Let your feelings set free and not suppress them anymore.

Sometimes it's good to let your soul rejoice and fly with the unexpressed emotions flowing inside you!

CHAPTER SEVEN

16th December 2013, 5:45 P.M.

I get off the college bus on my way back home. Slowly treading towards the house, my mind gets occupied with the thoughts of that same guy I had seen at the gym. I feel nervous even at the thought of going to the gym today.

"Why does he keep staring at me? Who is he? Do I know him?" I keep asking myself.

I walk upstairs to my room with those thoughts still buzzing in my mind. Keeping the college bag aside, I start looking around for clothes to wear to the gym. I wash my face, pull on an old green-colored t-shirt and white tracks with some pigeon print over it. With a water bottle and face towel in hand, I start jogging towards the gym.

I try to focus on my steps, despite the loud traffic noises interrupting my thoughts. When I reach the gym, I try to keep my face hidden under a towel while entering, pretending to wipe the sweat off my face. I look around, with the towel still covering the lower half of my face.

"Thank God! He is not here yet," I assure myself after sweeping a quick gaze across the gym.

Feeling relaxed, I keep my water bottle and towel aside and start with the warm-up. Walking slowly and steadily on the treadmill after that, I look at myself in the mirror right into my eyes when suddenly, someone crosses my sight in the same mirror. It's him, with a far more intense look this time.

I take a deep breath, get off the treadmill and start cycling at one extreme corner of the gym.

He is at the diagonally opposite corner, warming up.

"I have decided. Today, I'll ask him why he keeps staring at me like a jerk. Who is he? I'll talk to him today," I tell myself confidently.

I keep a watch on him. After finishing his warm up, he walks over to the water cooler to fill his bottle. I get off the cycling machine and rush to the water cooler too. He turns his head, looks at me approaching him and walks away with his bottle half filled.

"What the fuck?" I mumble.

"Sarah," Alex calls me just then.

"Ya. Coming, Alex."

"Today, we will do some chest workout on this machine," he continues to say while pointing towards another piece of iron with a driver like seat in the middle and two long rods with handles on both sides.

"What's that?" I ask him.

"We call it the butterfly machine," he tells me.

"Oh! Okay," I reply.

"Wait! I'll show you how to do it," he continues.

He sits on the driver-like seat, keeping his back straight against the long rod holding the weights. He stretches his arms a bit and slowly pulls both the handles on either side of the machine towards the front, applying pressure on his shoulders and chest.

He then asks me to repeat the same. Suddenly, he is summoned to the reception for a phone call.

"Hey! George. Could you please help her out with the butterfly machine?" Alex calls out to someone to assist me with the chest workout, as I was still fairly new to the gym. That someone was him. "George," I repeat his name to myself.

My heart starts to pound faster as he approaches me. Our gazes meet in an intense eye contact. This time, I don't want myself to be out of his sight. It feels like I have already dived deep into his heart through his breathtaking eyes, which carry gentleness and honesty within them. He is tall, strong and fair, yet so shy and sober in his demeanour. I find myself unable to appreciate just one thing about him. My gaze lingers all over him.

"44 pounds?" George asks me. His voice rings in my ears for the very first time.

"Umm, sorry?"

"I mean, would you be able to lift 44 pounds?" He bends down and starts adjusting the weights.

"No. That's too heavy for me," I speak out stressing more on my words.

He smiles at me and reduces the weights.

"22 pounds?" he asks again.

"NO!"

"5 pounds?" his voice becomes all the more polite.

"Yes, I'll try that," I concede.

He asks me to sit on the butterfly machine's bench, directing me to keep my feet flat on the floor.

"Place your forearms against the arm pads. Your forearms should be perpendicular to the floor and your upper arms parallel to the floor. Push against the arms hard enough to lift the weights off the stack. This is the starting point. Push against the weights till the butterfly arms almost touch in front of your chest. Keep your chest elevated, don't let it sink in. Pause for a count and then slowly lower back to the starting position," he says everything in one go.

"Umm, could you please be a bit slow?" I request.

"Ohh! Okay. Let's start again."

This time, he comes right in front of my face, while I am sitting on the bench and gives a slight support to the arm pads, so that I don't feel the machine's jerk on my arms. Very gently, he repeats every step with me. He is so close to me that I can smell him very well. A gush of sweet Cedrat fragrance fills my nostrils as he presses those arm pads closer to me.

"How many sets?" Alex jumps in.

"I don't know," I reply, feeling embarrassed.

"3 sets," George replies in my stead.

"That's all for today, girl," Alex tells me.

"Oh, okay. Should I leave then?" I ask.

"You can, after 2-3 sets of 10 crunches each," he says.

"OKAY!" I feel happy at the chance of staying for some more time at the gym.

"Umm, thank you!" I say to George in a soft voice.

He looks at me and addresses my gratitude with a smile.

After the crunches, I have no choice but to leave for home.

Before leaving, I try to catch a glimpse of George through the mirrors and find him looking at me. We share a smile again, but this time, a more familiar one. I walk out of the gym with a smile, never so prominent before. On my fifteen minutes' walk to my house, I find my mind occupied with the thoughts of George.

"George," I say and breathe out a deep sigh.

The colour of love is as pure and vibrant as that of a rainbow.

And if you ever get a chance to dip yourself into one,

Never walk your steps backwards.

CHAPTER EIGHT

17th December 2013, 6:15 P.M.

At the gym

"He is usually here by 6:10 P.M. Why hasn't he arrived yet?" I ask myself while doing the warm-up. My gaze is stuck at the entrance of gym. Every time I hear a bike's sound, I wish it to be him. I then jump to the treadmill and think of him looking at me through the mirror. I become anxious to know where he might be at this moment. I feel a sense of attachment towards him growing inside me. It feels like he has always belonged to me, since way before time started. I had hardly stopped thinking about him when I hear something.

"Hi!" I hear George's voice.

"Hi!" I wave at him with a smile.

A gush of happiness washes through me. His mere presence seems to have made my day. There is something between us, which I can't recognize at this moment. For the entire time that I am at gym, we converse only by looking at each other. I keep my gaze locked at him through those mirrors, while he catches sight of me every single moment too. I see him wrapping a bandage around his wrists before starting with his dumbbell squats or going to the locker room to get his drinks. I notice the way his lips move when he talks, the way he smiles, his habit of setting his hair every time they get sweaty. My eyes capture every move of his. This is the first time that I feel an inner voice telling me, "I belong to him."

I see him everywhere. Today I spend some half an hour more at the gym, only to see George for a bit longer.

"Sarah!" I suddenly hear my mom's voice.

I am shocked to see her here at the gym. I then remember that she had asked me that very morning to come home a bit early to help her out at the grocery store.

She stands at the reception and asks me to come off the treadmill. Nodding my head, I simply follow her out. Before I leave the gym however, I look back at George again in an attempt to silently tell him that I didn't want to go, but needed to leave at the moment. He blinks his eyes and smiles.

On our way to the store, mom keeps yelling and scolding me.

"You are good for nothing. You can't take on any responsibility properly. I don't know who will ever marry you. What were you doing for so long at the gym? Girls should not stay out for so long. You should help me out with the household chores instead of wasting money on such stupid activities. We are already paying for your studies, you should be grateful for that." She enters into an unstoppable mode of criticizing me.

I usually don't answer when I am forcefully dragged into an argument because at the end, I am the only one who is made to be the guilty party. All I do is just wait for it to get over. Perhaps once I start earning money, they'll change there thinking about me. The one thing that I want my parents to learn, is to treat their children with respect. On every birthday or anniversary of my parents, I save money out of my pocket to get them gifts or prepare greeting cards for them. I do all this out of my love and respect for them, but I get nothing except criticism and scolding in return. I don't remember the last time when my mom or dad gave me a hug out of love. Is it a sin to be a girl with big dreams? I get lost in self-assessment.

Soon, we reach the supermarket.

I drag out a trolley and move in with mom through the entrance.

"Milk, bread, broccoli…" I go over the grocery list. While my mother gets busy looking for vegetables and fruits, I slip into the cosmetics' section to get a face wash. As I pick up one and drop it in my trolley, I see George standing beside me.

"Hey! I am amazed to see you here," I say to him.

"Hey, ya! I just came in to buy some peanut butter," he replies.

"Oh, okay."

"So, what you doing here? Helping mom?"

"Yes, kind of. I need to rush, though. I shall talk to you later."

"Hmm. See ya. Take care."

"You too."

***

I rush to the billing counter. My mom is there already. We get the groceries billed and then walk back home. I wonder if George was stalking me. Even if he was, I loved it.

11:25 P.M.

Tucked in bed, I rest my laptop on my lap. Curious to know more about George, I type his name in the Facebook search.

"G.E.O.R.G.E. George. But what's his surname? Should I just type 'George Gurgaon'?" I keep mumbling while searching for his profile.

After a couple of consecutive searches, I finally find him.

"So, I have finally found you, Mr. George Smith."

I check out his entire profile. His college friends, his family photos and almost every post that he has made. He seemed pretty interesting. I see all of his pictures, the ones where he is modelling, playing the guitar, doing photography and being poetic as well.

"Cool!" I mumble to myself, shut the laptop down and fall sleep with his thoughts buzzing in my mind.

Not everyone can choose love.

Love chooses you.

You feel it within you,

Growing inch by inch every moment.

Leading you ultimately to another universe.

CHAPTER
NINE

18th December 2013, 9:00 P.M.

After the workout that day, I go to a nearby juice shop, as Alex had advised me to include juices in my diet. I order for a big glass of orange juice and stand near the counter. A bike suddenly comes swiftly towards me. As it draws closer, I realize that it is George.

He is here to have juice too, I think. I start smiling because I love it when he is around.

"What are you having?" he asks.

"Orange juice, as you can see," I reply dramatically.

I get butterflies in my belly whenever I see him. I wish I could just tell him. Maybe I should wait for some more time till I am more sure of my feelings. He comes to stand near me and starts a conversation.

"So, Sarah, what do you do?"

"I am pursuing my graduation in Computer Science."

"In Amity University?" he utters.

"How do you know?"

"Umm..I sent you a friend request on Facebook. I saw it on your profile there. Would you mind accepting it?"

"Uh! I haven't checked my profile since last week. I'll do it today," I lie.

Somewhere, I feel happy that I am a part of his thoughts too.

"Why did you join a gym then? Do you get enough time after college?"

"I feel I am very fat and that I should shed some weight to fit into my favorite clothes at least," I say sadly.

"No. Who says you need to shed weight? You look beautiful."

"Haha! Are you joking?"

"No, trust me, I am serious."

"Okay. If you say so."

We then start walking towards my home. Eventually, he accompanies me all the way. We keep talking the entire time.

"My house is just here. I think we should continue this tomorrow. Would you mind?" I say.

"No, it's perfectly alright. It felt nice talking to you," he says, a bit hesitantly.

"Same here." I wave at him and walk up to my room.

12:10 A.M.

I login to my Facebook account and search out his friend request. Indeed, he had sent me one. I accept it and send him a 'Hi' in his inbox. Little did I know that he was online already and was waiting for me to accept his request.

"Hey! Reached home safely?" he pinged back.

"Haha, obviously. You accompanied me back almost the entire way," I reply.

"So, what are you doing?"

"Nothing, just had dinner. Now talking to you."

"Can we exchange numbers?"

I pause for a while to wonder whether he was actually a stalker.

"Should I give him my number?" I mumble to myself.

"I don't have a personal phone. I use my mom's if I need to call someone," I lie to him.

"Okay," he replies after 7 minutes of silence.

In the meantime, my notification box fills up with notifications by George Smith.

George Smith likes a photo of yours.

George Smith likes a photo you are tagged in.

George Smith likes a post of yours.

Shocked completely, I text him back, "Hey! My notification box is full of your name."

"Yeah, I was liking all your pictures. All of them are so pretty, specially the one in which you are wearing those cute feather earrings."

"Thanks! That is very sweet of you," I text back, turning completely blank.

That whole night, he keeps liking my pictures dropping comments over them. At 4:15 A.M. we were both still online.

"Good morning!" I text him.

"What! I didn't realize," he says.

"Neither did I. I think I will sleep for sometime, till we meet at the gym later today," I reply to him.

"Okay! As you say."

"☺"

"☺"

I am hurt, and you feel the pain.

I rejoice and you feel the rain.

This story of love is always short of expression,

But only the one who holds it can well explain.

CHAPTER TEN

25th December 2013, 6:10 P.M.

Christmas Eve

As days pass by, George and I spend more and more time talking to each other at the juice shop or texting on Facebook, trying to know more of each other. We soon become good friends. However, I haven't shared my number with him yet, neither has he asked me for it again.

I didn't go to college that day. There weren't many lectures scheduled for that day, as half of our class' strength was busy with Christmas celebrations, and the rest had planned a mass bunk. Waiting for the clock to hit 6:00 P.M., I get ready for the gym. Suddenly however, I receive my mother's call.

"Sarah, where are you?" she asks. She wasn't at home as she had gone out with my brother for some shopping.

"At home, but I was about to step out for the gym," I say.

"Well, could you join us at the Church? Danish and I are waiting here. We have a lot of stuff to carry and Danish wants to meet his friends here."

"Sure, I am coming." With no other option in sight, I agree to my mom's request and join her at Saint Michael's Church, which is right behind the juice shop I usually go to.

I run all the way to the church, almost breathless with the effort, but I don't want to get late for the gym. I help my mom with the load of shopping bags and then light a candle at the church with my brother for Jesus. We are not Christian by religion, but I love to visit Churches during Christmas. They are always so beautifully decorated. After spending almost an hour at the church, I tell my mom that I need to rush to the gym.

"Oh, God! What will you do there now? It's so late already," my mother screams.

"I'll be back in an hour or so," I insist.

"Okay. But not later than that," she concedes.

"Okay," I assure her.

I run back towards the gym. As I enter, I see George standing right next to the reception.

"Where have you been?" he asks spontaneously.

"Ah! I was at the church with mom," I reply while entering my attendance in the register.

"I have been waiting for you," he continues.

"What for?" I ask back, pretending to be completely unaware.

"Nothing, just wanted to start the workout once you joined in."

"Aww! That's so sweet," I mock at him.

We were both well aware of our feelings for each other, however, we hadn't confessed it yet. I started going to the gym everyday, just to see him. I began to feel as if he had already become a part of me. While I am about to finish my workout, George summons me near the water cooler. He doesn't call out, but simply requests to do so with a gesture.

"Yes? Why did you call me like that?" I laugh at him.

"Nothing. Just needed a favor," he says.

"Favor? From me? Tell me, what can I do?"

"Will you go to the Church with me?"

"Umm! What?" I turn blank.

"Ya. I haven't ever been to the Church, neither have any of my friends ever gone there. I, myself, don't know why, but today I really want to visit it with you! Will you please just accompany me there?" I see something different in his eyes as he says it.

"Ya! Sure. Let's go then." I feel happy at the opportunity of getting some quite time with him.

He smiles at me again, as if I have given him the joy of his life.

"I need to reach home by 9:00 P.M. today. Let's walk a bit faster," I tell him as we walk towards the church.

"Okay, as you say." He looks at me, smiles again and bobs his head on either side.

"Are you fine?" I ask him.

"Absolutely. What would happen to me?"

"I don't know, you look a little different today."

"Ahh! You will get to know."

Finally, we reach the Church and buy a candle each. As we move in, I keep telling him about how much I like going to the church and the peace of mind I get from being there. As I keep talking, I notice his eyes constantly holding my gaze. Both of us kneel at the altar, light our candles and I observe him making his wish to Jesus.

"What did you pray for?" I ask him, turning curious.

"I will let you know once Jesus listens to it."

"Okay."

As we walk halfway back from the Church, we chance upon a very isolated street.

"I can't see anyone else besides us here. This place is so…"

"So isolated…" he whispers, drawing very close to me. I can feel his soft lips grazing softly over my ears. Slipping his hand into mine and entangling my fingers with his own, he pulls me towards himself with a force I can't withstand. I am pulled close enough to feel his warm breath all over my lips and neck.

"Sarah!" He whispers my name in my ears and hugs me tightly.

"George? What happened?" I ask him as I move one of my hands through his neck and into his hair, while resting the other right over his heart. My eyes dive deep into his and our bodies press close against each other, enough to not let anything through.

"You. You happened to me Sarah!" he whispers softly, while our arms are still around each other and our eyes dive deep into each other's souls.

"There's not a single moment when I don't think about you. I have already lost my heart to you since our gazes crossed each other for the very first time. Today, I asked you to come here with me not just because I wanted you to accompany me to the church, but because I want you to accompany me at every step of my life from now on. You asked me what I was praying to Jesus for. I prayed to have you in my life. I don't know what you feel for me, but I want you to know that I love you. I have loved you since the first time I saw you and I will love you beyond infinite boundaries. I promise you that I'll always be there with you my entire life and even in all my further lives."

He pauses and looks at me with those intimidating eyes.

Sarah, do you…?"

"I love you George…I love you," I speak out, interrupting his words and hug him even more tightly. "I feel the same for you too, but couldn't gather the courage to confront you, afraid of how you might react. I come to the gym everyday just to see you and then I think about you for the rest of the day. Jesus has not just listened to your prayer, but to both of ours," I continue to say, getting teary eyed.

He wipes the tears trickling down my checks and draws even more close, as I feel his breath more prominently over my face. He moves his hand slowly to my neck and un-ties my hair, while his other hand continues to hold me tightly at my back. The cold breeze grows somewhat warm around us. Slowly, our lips get locked with each other, his tongue starts playing around my lower lip and his eyelashes roll over mine. He drops a shower of kisses all over my neck, lips, and cheeks, as his hold on me grows even tighter. He then holds my face in both his hands and plants a kiss on my forehead.

"I love you," he finally says.

"I love you, George."

This day, two bodies turned into one soul.

I don't talk much to everyone,
'Cause it takes a while for me to understand them.
But with you, it feels like I am exploring my own self.

CHAPTER ELEVEN

25th December 2013, 11:10 P.M.

"Hi :* sweetheart!" George texts me.

"I was just about to text you, dear :*," I reply.

"I can't believe Jesus actually listened to my prayer. Holding you in my arms and saying all that to you still feels like a dream to me," George continues to type.

"Haha! I can't tell you how nervous I had been to talk to you about this. But see, things turned out so beautifully, that I had never imagined before. I am so happy for us."

I pause for a while and start typing again.

"8745-----7"

"Whoa! You finally shared your number," he replies all excitedly.

"Haha! Yes, finally."

"Can I call you now?"

"Not now. Mom and dad are around. I'll give you a call in some time."

After around 15-20 minutes, I give George a call and we talk about almost everything in our lives; be it family, childhood memories, our college and office issues and every other piece of non-sense. He cracks a joke and I follow with a long laughter. No page from our lives went by which we didn't discuss, I guess.

"George! It's 5:00 A.M...." I say, completely surprised.

"What? Really?"

"Yes, we spent the entire night talking again."

"Lets get some sleep then...haha. You have your lectures tomorrow, right?" he asks.

"Yes. Good night then.."

"Good morning, Sarah. Love you."

"Love you too <3."

As I put down the phone, a thought creeps into my mind and gets me completely nervous. George and I surely love each other a lot, but will I ever be able to confront my family about this. They didn't even allow me to decide my college trips myself. Will they ever allow me to take my life's biggest decision on my own?

"Maybe, this is not the right time to tell them," I say to myself.

"I should first complete my studies and get a good job. Maybe then they'll think of me as a mature person, capable of taking my own decisions. I think, I should wait for some more time."

Promises don't need witnesses,

They need your own commitment to self.

These are strong bonds, yet fragile.

So once you make them,

do keep them through all the mile.

CHAPTER TWELVE

27th December 2013, 6:12 A.M.

I wake up to a sudden buzz on my phone.

"Good morning, my sweet love :*," he texts.

"Good morning baby :*."

"Movie ;) ?" he asks me out.

A smile comes to my face.

"Umm, okay."

"Cool! I'll catch you at the bus stop. Don't you dare get on the college bus. Haha! ;)"

"Haha! I'll wait for your Harley. Don't worry. ;)"

I put on a long grey colored dress with some white zigzag pattern on it. Matching it with a pair of black boots, I put on a decent eyeliner and a nude shade of lipstick. After all, it's our first date. I can feel the butterflies in my belly. Suddenly, everything starts feeling so beautiful. Happiness surrounds me like never before. There is a strange beautiful feeling, which mere words can't express. Looking at myself in the mirror for the thousandth time, I tidy up every strand of my hair and finally get ready.

I reach the bus stop exactly at 7:48 A.M.

"Where are you? I am already at the bus stop," I call to say to him.

"Me too!" I hear his voice coming from behind me. In a light yellow sweatshirt and a black leather jacket, my eyes get stuck on him yet again. We give each other a tight hug.

"I want all my mornings to start with your hug," he speaks softly in my ears. I smile at him and say, "Soon, this will happen too."

We then ride away to our destination. While he is driving, he slips both my hands into the pockets of his leather jacket, so that my hands don't get cold and I lean over his back with my eyes closed. I feel so protected with him. There is so much understanding and calmness in every move of his. It feels like he already knows what's going on in my mind and what I need. In not more than twenty minutes, we reach the Ambience Island, Gurgaon.

"Excuse me, ma'am." The security person stops us.

"Yes?"

"The mall is closed," he replies.

"What? But it's a weekday," George says.

"Sir, I mean to say that the mall opens around 10:00 A.M."

"Oh!" George and I look at each other for a moment and then burst into laughter. We sit at the bench outside the mall gate and start talking about the beautiful weather outside.

“Its so beautiful out here. Look at the sky, so calm and sober,” I say.

“Yes! But not any more than you.”

“Oh! Is it?”

“Yeah! Okay, listen. I’ll just get back.”

“Where are you going?”

“You’ll find out soon enough.”

He runs towards the highway and then turns somewhere to the left. After a few minutes I see him coming back with a big cup of steaming hot tea.

“You can really read my mind. I was just thinking about and had started to crave for some hot tea in this cold weather.”

“See, I came to know,” he replies with a smile.

We share the same cup of tea and start talking about how we used to check each other out at the gym through all those mirrors around us. We talk about everything all the time, yet somehow we never run out of words. I feel so good with him. He is so honest, so understanding and so caring. He has already woven our future in his mind. He tells me how he imagines me dressed like a bride on our wedding day, my opening the door for him when he gets back from work, waking up beside him every morning and going to bed with him every night. I can see everything very clearly in his eyes too.

“Please come in, sir, ma’am.” The security guard calls out to us, as he sees us waiting outside.

“Finally!” George says.

We move in and start to discuss which movie to watch. After almost half an hour, we buy two tickets for the last seats of the cinema hall. We had chosen a romantic thriller to watch. George buys a big bucket of popcorn and we walk inside. We whisper in each other's ears about the scenes in the movie, its cast and the plot. We get close enough and slowly find ourselves lost in our own world.

"I love you," he says softly to me.

"I love you, George," I reply back.

We spend the entire day together. George then takes me to a jewellery shop and asks me to buy anything that I might like.

"No! It's very expensive. I'll buy something some other time," I say.

George hands me his wallet and insists that I buy something, but I don't. After a few minutes, he holds my hand and slips a beautiful ring onto my ring finger. It has a beautifully carved pink rose with pearls and diamonds studded on it in Italian design.

"I can't think of enough words to tell you what you mean to me. With this ring, however, I want to say that you are my love, my wife and my everything." He holds both my hands in his and kisses them. I hold his hands much tighter and give him a hug.

"I love you so much, my sweet husband." Exchanging vows in unheard whispers, we quietly get married to each other in our hearts.

All of me is you and all of you is me.

So come, let's get along on the journey of love and get mesmerised in this quite breeze around.

CHAPTER THIRTEEN

7th February, 2014.

Time passes and we grow even more close to each other. George introduces me to his mother and his aunt. I start visiting his home and begin interacting with his family members more frequently. George had lost his father when he was ten years old. After the tragic incident, his mother single handedly brought him up. After a few years, George's aunt brought him and his mother to Gurgaon and asked them to stay with her, thereby providing them with all the comfort and mental support they needed. George has successfully completed his graduation in Electronics Engineering in first division from Gurgaon itself and is now working with a renowned MNC.

Whenever I visit George, his mom makes me a good cup of coffee and loads me with lots of things to eat. She is very sweet and simple.

It is the 7th of Feb, which marks the beginning of the Valentine's Week. It's Rose Day and I get very sweet Rose Day wishes from George, but I am upset because we won't meet today, as he is occupied with some office work, for which he is required to rush to Bangalore for two days. I get ready for college, as usual.

"Hey, sweetheart! I'm sorry I couldn't meet you today ☹," he texts me in the middle of my lecture.

"It's okay. You can't avoid office urgencies," I say, pretending to be fine. The whole day passes by and I keep thinking about him. In the evening as I am about to reach my house, George asks me to buy some sweets for him from a nearby sweet shop. As I enter the shop, somebody reaches out from behind to close my eyes. I recognise his touch and smell his fragrance.

"George!" I shout out with joy.

"Happy Rose Day, my sweet wife." He gives me a beautiful rose and hugs me.

"You almost made me cry!"

"Ohh! Really? I thought you would love to see me."

"Of course, I am happy. I have been thinking about you the whole day. See, I even got this for you," I say and give him a rose too.

"That's lovely," he says, smiling at me.

While everything goes smoothly, a fear captures my mind suddenly. A strange feeling overcomes my conscience. Little did I know that something unexpected was coming our way.

Sometimes the mind wanders amidst familiar thoughts.
Sometimes it gets lost on its own accord.
Try to listen to what the conscience has to say,
It might be the beginning of a new ray.

CHAPTER FOURTEEN

10th February 2014

While getting back from college, I get a message from George. "Dinner tonight?"

"Okay. I'll de-board the bus halfway. You can pick me up then."

"Sure. Call me when you are about to reach."

"Cool!"

Halfway to my house, I give him a call and de-board the bus. He arrives there on his bike. I take the back seat and hold him tight. He drives me towards a nearby restaurant.

"I have to reach home early today," I tell him.

"Why? All good?"

"I don't know. I have been having this weird feeling for the last two or three days. I think we should not meet so frequently. My parents might get to know about us and I don't want them to discover all this the wrong way."

"Sweetheart! One day, we'll need to confront them about our love anyway, so why not today? They might get angry at first, but they'll eventually accept us," he says.

"Yaar! You don't know my parents, they would rather kill me if they come to know of all this. I don't know, I feel very scared. I constantly have this feeling that someone is following us."

"Don't worry! I am always with you. Don't get so tensed. Leave all the tensions to me and just calm down, things will definitely turn out to be good. Have faith in our love and in me."

"I do have faith in us. I just want things to go smoothly." I lean against his back and close my eyes as he drives us across the city.

After about fifteen or twenty minutes, we finally reach the restaurant.

"So, what would my wife like to eat?"

"Chinese!"

"Cool. One plate Hakka noodles with Manchurian. Please keep the gravy thick," he places the order.

I constantly keep biting my lip. George can see that I am getting restless.

"Bubbu! What are you thinking now?" He tries to calm me down. He calls me Bubbu out of love.

"Umm! Nothing much. I told you na, I am kinda getting some negative vibes these days."

"Do you remember the first time our eyes crossed and we lost our hearts to each other?"

"Yes! How can I ever forget that?"

"Were you scared of loving me the very first time you saw me?"

"No…"

"Then why should we be scared of confessing our love to our parents? They want us to be happy too. Trust me, everything will turn out to be good. Let's have dinner now."

After talking to George, I feel at peace. He is right, I feel. I should just remain calm and God will definitely sort things out for us.

After having dinner, George and I walk towards the road to my house. We talk about the big bright moon over us, how quiet it is, how the moonlight scatters all around us, those stars twinkling in the night sky and the sweet breeze around us. As we walk along the abandoned street, George slips my hand to his waist.

"Hey! What's that?" I ask George, turning completely blank.

"Get to know yourself," he smiles.

A cute, brown teddy bear suddenly appears from within his jacket.

"Happy Teddy Day, Bubbu…" he continues, with a smile growing all the more wide on his face. I wish him back with that furrybone wrapped around me.

"But…" I take a long pause.

"But?"

"How will I be able to take it home? My mom will see it and you how things will turn out further."

"Ah! How will she even come to know about it? And even if she does, just speak the truth and tell her that I gave this to you."

"Speak the truth? Do you even know what you are saying? My parents will kill me if they see this suddenly appear in my room, that too during Valentines' Week." George can see what got me so tensed.

"I don't know, you'll have to take this home. Trust me, if anything goes wrong, I am always here by your side," George insists and I hide the teddy in my bag, pushing it down and covering it with my scarf.

George books a cab for me. While we wait for it to arrive, he does not let go of my hand and gives me a kiss on the forehead, asking me not to worry at all.

After reaching back home, I make my way to my room quietly and lock the door from inside. I then try to find a good place to hide that furry little thing.

"Sarah?" My mother calls out as soon as she hears the sound of my footsteps coming from the room.

"Ya, mom. Coming. Just changing my clothes."

"Why did you get in so late today? I need to talk to you. Come here as soon as you are done with the changing," she commands.

Getting even more hasty, I open my cupboard and hide the teddy bear under a heap of clothes in the lower drawer. Before leaving the room, I reassure myself that everything is looking normal around me. Preparing myself for the upcoming thunder, I walk over to my mom's room to find out what she wanted to talk about.

"Why did you come in so late today?" she asks directly.

"Actually, the bus got stuck in traffic. That's why."

"Are you sure?"

"Ya! You can ask my bus-mates."

"Okay. Make some tea till I get back from my friend's place."

"Sure!"

I feel relieved that she didn't ask anymore questions. Somewhere in the back of my mind, however, I could sense a ball of trouble rolling towards me. Recalling George's words, I decide to not overthink it and just prepare myself for the upcoming cultural fest at the college.

Have faith, 'cause all you are going through will end one day.

Have faith, 'cause not all your days will remain the same.

God has already planned something for everyone,

And yours' too will reach you soon!

CHAPTER FIFTEEN

13th February, 2014. 10:40 A.M.

After several requests and pleas to the HOD, I get the chance to do a solo dance performance for not more than two minutes in duration. There's hardly any space in my room, even to make a full twirl. Therefore, I decide to do all my practice during college hours, that too in the free lecture theatres.

"Hey! Are you Sarah?" A guy whom I had never met before, calls me out in the college corridor.

"Umm, yes. But, I don't recognize you."

"Hi, I'm Jeff from the Cultural Affairs Department."

"Nice to meet you, Jeff. How come you have crossed my path like this today?"

"You have a solo dance performance on the 14th Feb. Right?"

"Don't tell me the HOD has cancelled it."

"No. The performance has not been cancelled, but preponed."

"What? When? Why didn't I get any calls for this?"

"It has been rescheduled for today."

"No way. How can you guys do that? I haven't even prepared completely yet," I yell at him with both of my hands over my head. "I don't even have the dress!" I continue yelling.

"Sorry! But you'll have to manage. The performances with start around 4:00 P.M. All the best." Jeff runs away, leaving me completely annoyed.

I dial up George and vomit out everything to him.

"Should I come to your college? We can buy a new dress from a nearby store," he suggests.

"But I don't have that much time."

After thinking hard for a while, I finally ask George if he could pick up the dress from my house. I am aware that I was putting my head in the chopper's bucket with this act, but somewhere in my heart, I knew that I already had enough strength to confront my parents about our love story.

"Are you okay, my boy?" George asks, not believing what I had just said.

"Yes. I am okay and I want you to meet my mom." My voice shakes a bit as I say these words.

"Should I tell her about us?" he teases.

"No…no. Just tell her that we are colleagues."

Gathering my guts, I call my mom and inform her about George.

"Who is coming?" I imagine my mom raising her ears as she utters this.

“George, my colleague.”

“You’ve never told me about him.”

“I met him just a few days ago.”

“Okay. Where is your costume, by the way?”

“It’s inside my cupboard.”

George knows my address as he lives nearby. Many a times when we are unable to talk to each other, he asks me to come out to the balcony, so he can look at me. We look at each other and do the talking in sign language. It’s funny, yet beautiful.

Around 2:50 P.M., I get a call from George.

“Hey, my boy! I got the costume.”

“What? Where are you? Can you come to the cafeteria?”

I watch him in disbelief as he approaches me with a smile on his face.

“How did your meeting with my mom go?”

“It was good. She asked me to come back for a cup of tea.”

“Are you kidding me? She invited you for tea? Impossible.” My mind starts reeling.

“Yes, she did. I even touched her feet and she seemed happy.”

“That’s weird…I think, I’ll have a blast at home tonight. Wish me luck.”

“Hahah. You look cute when you pass on such PJs.”

George thinks I am cracking jokes, but little does he know that something horrifying is waiting for me back home. My instinct tells me so.

I call up my mom to assess her mood, but surprisingly she sounds happy. This confuses me even more.

George and I then head towards the college auditorium where my performance is to be held.

"Wish me luck!" I look up at George and hold his hands.

He hugs me tight and wishes me well for an amazing performance. As I knew it would, the performance goes way better than I had expected. The crowd continues to cheer me on till I get off the stage. Among all those claps and cheers, I could clearly hear a much louder and distinct whistling and cheering, which was sustained right from the beginning of the performance, till the time I got down from the stage. George appeared to be no less than a school boy.

"Woohooo! You were amazing, my wifey." He wraps his arms around me.

"Thank you!" My smile gets wider and wider as he unloads lots of kisses over me.

After spending the rest of the day at the fest, George drops me off near my house. He kisses me on my forehead and I walk back to my house with a million questions striking my mind.

"So, how was the performance?" my mother asks me, staring me down from top to toe.

"Yes! It was very nice," I reply back to her while hastily pulling clips out of my hair, while my voice gets stuck in my throat.

"Give me your phone," she says, snatching my phone from my hands, and investigates through my photo gallery. A few days back, she had seen a picture in my phone, where a woman was taking a sneek-peek into the shorts of a man. She had then told this whole thing in a much-exaggerated manner to dad. I tired myself telling them that some idiot guy from my class had shared that picture on the college WhatsApp group and that I had nothing to do with the picture, but there is no medicine for doubt.

Since I know this habit of my mom of presenting everything in an exaggerated manner to my dad, I simply prepare myself for the drama which is about to take place when dad comes back home in the evening. As expected, mom starts talking to dad about George.

"You know what happened today?" My mom says to dad as he kicks off his shoes and takes a seat near the dining table.

"What?"

"I told you, this girl has slipped out of our hands. Now she has started making boyfriends."

A drop of sweat trickles down my forehead and my heart starts thumping loudly with nervousness, as I hear my mom starting the conversation.

"Unknown guys have now started coming to our house. No doubt, she will call them home in our absence someday and will do whatever she wants with them," my mom continues without giving the slightest thought to what impression my dad might make of me from her words.

"Sarah…" my dad calls out to me, turning completely red.

I walk towards the dining area with short steps, turning completely blank in my mind.

"What the hell is this? I am sending you to college to study, not to make boyfriends. You should be grateful to us that we are at least giving you education. Otherwise, we would have gotten you married to some worker by now. BITCH!"

My dad keeps yelling at me and says all these words which no dad is supposed to say to his daughter. With my head bowed down, I simply just listen to him without a single retort.

Adding on to this drama, my mom opens my cupboard, takes the teddy bear out and hands it to my dad.

"See this. She even asked that guy George to gift her a teddy bear," she tells my dad with a disgusted look on her face.

"Bloody whore!" My dad gives me a tight slap on my face and throws the teddy to one corner of the room. He slaps me so hard that I fall onto a chair nearby. I prepare myself for the worst to happen.

"Are we not earning enough to buy you such cheap stuff. Besides, are you of the age to play with such toys anymore…?" He comes closer to me and continues to abuse me with words that I have never heard before. My mom just continues to look at me with her hands folded and does nothing to calm my father down. Instead, she ignites him even more with her words.

"Let me teach you how a girl should behave," he says as he draws even closer to me. With his left hand he takes hold of my hair and continues to slap my face with his other hand till I stop feeling the pain and turn completely numb.

"This girl has no respect for us. Trust me, the day is not far when she'll insult us in front of the whole society," my mother continues to poke my dad. Under the influence of her words, my dad sways me forcefully from one side to the other, his left hand still wrapped tightly around my hair. I can feel some of the hair on my head pulling out from my scalp, under the forceful pressure of the father's hand. Neither does my mother stop, nor does he. My brother moves to the next room as soon as he sees this. Within this closed room, I am beaten, thrashed to the ground, slapped innumerable times and my soul is torn down with words so terrible, that I feel ashamed even to be alive.

Suddenly, I stop feeling my body. I stop feeling the pain on my scalp, the bruises on my face and body.

Numbness takes over me completely and all I can think about in that moment, is George.

Whatever happens, happens for a reason.

There is a cause behind every incident.

We don't realise it until the picture gets more clear.

CHAPTER SIXTEEN

14th February, 2014. 08:20 A.M.

I sit in my room the whole night, thinking about all that had happened and all that was said. I skip my college the next morning, as I don't want people to make fun of me on seeing my swollen eyes and bruised hands, but feel the urge to talk to George and tell him that things are not going good. I dial up George after carefully slipping the phone away from my mom's pillow-side.

"Hey!"

"Saraah? Where are you? I had been trying to call you, but your number was constantly not reachable. Have you missed the bus today? Should I come to pick you up?" George says, his voice full of concern.

"Hang on, George, and listen carefully. Things are not going too good at my place. Nothing is happening right and it's getting worst by the minute. Please don't call or text me till you receive my word. Wait for my call. Love you!"

"But….tell me what happened?"

“I told you, wait for my call.”

“Okay, I’ll wait for your call and yes, I love you. Happy Valentine’s Day, wifey.” George’s voice turns softer.

The whole day, I am ordered around to do household chores and am made to remember what my position is. A girl is not allowed to do things her way as it is seen as an insult to her upbringing by her parents. I am told repeatedly how the daughters of my uncle are far more mannered and disciplined than I am.

“Do you know how quite and intelligent that girl Anu is? She has never raised her voice in front of her parents. Whatever her parents say, she follows quietly and never questions them. I wonder where we failed in your upbringing. All this non-sense called LOVE is a piece of shit and don’t you dare to be over-smart with us. You’ll get married exactly where I want you to, and not where you think you would,” my mother keeps uttering this to me as I do the dishes. With every word of hers, my eyes drop a tear of shame. Shame, that despite being a topper at my college and earning so many awards and recognitions for my parents, I had failed to earn respect in my own house.

What is the use of studying so hard and thinking about your parents so much, when you are not even given basic respect by them in return. Is being a girl that shameful? I never failed to appreciate them and make them realize how special they were to me, but unfortunately, all that has been of no worth. A girl is considered to be characterless the day she decides to follow her heart. No matter how qualified she is, or how much she values her family, a single decision to make her own choices makes her a whore.

"I am going out with your dad for some work. Make sure the laundry is done before I get back. Idiot!" My mother slams the door behind her and walks out with my dad. Dad gives me a look so disgusting before leaving that I already feel ashamed of being his daughter.

As both of them move out, I lock the door and run towards the store room, sit down there with my back resting against the wall and cry out loud. Thinking about all the past memories, my eyes roll up and down, gazing at the dark walls of the storeroom. I curse myself for being the way I am. Suddenly, the phone rings; it's George.

"Hey..?" George says from the other side.

"I told you to wait for my call…why can't you…I…" I stutter and then start crying over the call.

"Sarah? What happened, tell me? Why are you crying? Is everything all right?" George gets tensed.

I explain everything to him, all that had happened the previous day and how I am being treated.

"This should not happen, Sarah. This is not right. I want to meet you. Now! I can't let all this happen to you."

"You can't do anything about it. This is not the first time that it is happening. I have already told you what my family is like."

"Listen Sarah, I don't care how your family is, but now, you are my family, my everything. I can't see you like this. Can we please meet today? I am feeling very restless. I want to see you. Please?"

"Sorry, George, it is not possible today. I'll see you on Monday."

"No. You have an off tomorrow and the day after tomorrow as well. How will I be able to stay without seeing you for two long days?"

"George, I told you, it won't be possible for me. Things will turn even worse."

George sighs.

"Can you at least come to the balcony?" George insists.

"Yes…"

"But please don't disconnect the call."

"Okay."

Within the next two minutes, George arrives in his car on the busy street near my house. He parks his car there and looks at me through the car's window. I hear his breath over the call and he hears mine. We keep looking at each other and say nothing. I feel his sight already diving into mine and all I can feel is his immense love enveloping me.

A person's mind runs after happiness and peace.

And once it is found, he wants to stay by its side forever.

CHAPTER SEVENTEEN

17th February, 2014. 08:20 A.M.

I am dying to meet George. I had already texted him this morning to board the bus with me, but he hasn't arrived yet. I dial up his number.

"Where are youuu? It's 7:50 already," I literally start yelling at him.

"Sorry baby! I woke up late today. Will join you at college. Sorry," he says, his voice growing deeper.

"It's okay. I'll be waiting for you." I feel disappointed.

I board the bus at my stop and move towards the seats at the far rear. As I start hopping towards the back, somebody pulls my bag towards the right with a light jerk.

"George?" My eyes twinkle and I give myself up to him.

"I have been missing you so badly, my wifey!" He squeezes me in his arms, with his beard rubbing over my cheeks. For the entire journey, I rest my head on his shoulder, cry with him and laugh with him. I tell him every bit of my story and he quietly listens to me as if he has been waiting to hear every pain and every joy of my soul. As we reach college, we make our way to the cafeteria and get ourselves something to eat.

“I can still see the bruises on your face. How many times did your father slap you?” he asks, brushing his fingers lightly over my cheek.

“You think I was counting?” I laugh at him.

“I won’t let this happen to you again.”

“You can’t do anything, George.”

“Let’s get married.”

“Are you serious? I haven’t even graduated yet. You’ll have to wait for a couple more years,” I wink at him.

“I think we are going to get married soon.”

“Haha! Why not?”

“Listen, Sarah. I can’t let you face all this all alone. Both of us love each other, then why is it only you who has to be criticized for everything?”

“George, my family is just like that. I have already told you how conservative they are. I have grown habitual to going through all this now.”

“But I am not.”

A silence persists around us. George makes himself amply clear that he doesn’t want to see me in this condition ever again. We stroll around the college stadium for the rest of the day, then move to a farmhouse there and then to the library. In the evening, we board the same college bus on our way back home.

“I don’t want to go home now,” I whisper in his ears.

“Then don’t go. Stay with me forever, just like this, tangled in my arms and never going away.”

“I wish that day comes soon.”

He gives me a kiss on my forehead and I de-board the bus at my stop.

On my walk back home, George’s words keep reverberating in my mind.

Keep your eyes wide open,

'Cause you don't know when you catch a sight of the sunshine.

Keep your ears open,

'Cause you don't know when you get to hear the lifestyle music!

CHAPTER EIGHTEEN

10th March, 2014. 00:00 A.M.

"A very very happy birthday to my darling wifey."

"Hahaha! Thank you so much, my hubby."

"So, what's the plan for tomorrow?"

"Nothing much. I will go to college and then back home. That's the only plan I can think of."

"What if I make it happening?"

"And how would you do that?"

"Time will tell, my darling."

He must have something going on in his mind, I think to myself. I pull out the best suit I can find in my wardrobe, as I know somewhere in my mind that George would see me today. Mom and dad wish me birthday with a very faint heart. Unsure of what I can do to make them happy, I just touch their feet, hoping that everything would get better with time and pray to God for the same to happen.

Little did I know that George had already asked my bus mates to arrange a big cake for me. As I enter the bus the next morning, friends and folks shower me with the most wonderful wishes and praises. However, the face I want to see first isn't here yet.

On reaching college, I find George already waiting for me at the cafeteria.

"How can you look so beautiful?"

He makes me blush every time.

"It's not me, but the beauty in your eyes…"

"Haha! Turning philosophical, haan?"

"So, what's the plan for today?"

"Firstly, let's cut the cake, we will decide then."

He brings forth a big black forest cake, along with some of my friends from college. All my bus mates and friends have already come to know George and are very welcoming towards him. Actually, George is so nice himself that nobody can resist being touched by his charm and good nature. One of the many things which made me fall for George, is his compassion towards others. He knows the power of kindness, humanity and gratitude very well. I feel so lucky to have him as my entire universe.

"Why are you staring at me like that Bubbu?" he murmurs.

"Lets cut the cake," my friends start shouting.

I am loaded with best wishes and hugs. George isn't able to resist painting my face with the icing on the cake. Once everybody disperses for their classes, George holds my hand and takes me out on his bike.

"So, what's next?" My voice makes way to his ears against the wind, while we are on the bike.

He just nods his head up and down, gesturing that I should wait for what is coming.

On reaching our destination, I realise that he has brought me to the same church where we first confessed our love for each other in front of God. He makes me walk into the church as if it's our wedding day. He takes my arm in his and my sight rests unwaveringly on his face. He holds my hand up, moves his fingers over mine and slips on a beautiful ring studded with diamonds and pearls. He then presses me close to his heart and gives me a kiss on the forehead.

I have no words to say. All I can do is to keep looking at him with tears in my eyes. We actually don't need words to describe our love for each other. I spend the entire day with George. We wander around the city, eat at the street stalls and feel the cool breeze during our the long rides on his bike. What else does one need? We all have the hunger for love, compassion and gratitude, and the moment we find it, we must never let it go. There are very few people in this world who find their true love and even fewer are able to take a stand for it.

Staying with George gives me immense happiness. There is no time of the day when I'm not thinking about him; he is always present in every corner of my mind. I feel him with me all the time, even my clothes bear only his smell. He talks to me about every damn thing in my life, encourages me for what I want to do and appreciates me for who I am. No matter what, his support is constantly with me and that's what gives me strength. I had never thought that with a mere eye contact with him, I would lose my entire self to him. Maybe, this is the true meaning of love.

Somebody has rightly said, “Love liberates, and not binds.”

He has freed me from the captivity I had been living in for so long.

George never calls me his girlfriend; rather, he straight-away calls me his wife. He discusses all his problems with me, every thought that crosses his mind, all his troubles and sorrows. He is an open book in front of me.

We have already started making financial plans for our future, our kids, the furniture in our house, and every other minor thing. My birthday had never been so beautiful and happening.

“Thank you, George,” I say to him, as he drops me near my house.

“Thank you? For what? You are my wife and I’ll make every one of your birthdays as precious as I can.”

I wrap my arms around him and say I love you.

He holds me even tighter and his lips take control of me.

Never get influenced by what society says to you.

As many advices, as the mouths.

Follow your heart and listen to the most prominent voice.

'Cause, it isn't going to let you down.

CHAPTER NINETEEN

14th May, 2014. 04:00 P.M.

During my college summer vacations, I get myself enrolled for a Core JAVA Development programme at NIIT Gurgaon. It wasn't easy. I had to request my parents innumerable times, listen to their taunts, literally beg in front of them and what not I had to go through to get their consent. But finally, I saved some money and got myself enrolled in the course. Sometimes, George comes to visit me here too. There is a guy named Arav in my batch here. He turned out to be my college mate whom I didn't know and is my junior in the same course. During my JAVA classes, he often comes to me to discuss some technical concepts and some casual college stuff.

"So, done with today's stuff?" Arav joins me in the classroom after the lecture gets over.

"Yeah! Almost done. Just winding up with the notes," I say to him, while scribbling down the missing notes.

"Have you also started planning for the final project which you'll need to present to the faculty at college?"

"Oh! I completely forgot. Things are so messed up these days; so many assignments, classes, and then this project. I'll see when I will start with that too."

I pack my bag, hastily putting in my books, as I receive a text message from George saying that he is coming to see me. I wait for him at the reception. While I wait for him, Arav keeps wandering here and there at the reception, stealing glances at me sometimes, or giving me a smile.

After a while, the door opens and George enters. We both sit at the reception and talk for some good fifteen to thirty minutes.

"I need to buy some books, yaar. But mom dad is not even talking to me properly since that incident. I have only 200 bucks left with me."

"Keep it," George hands me his debit card.

"No! I can't take it," I tell George, giving his card back.

"Why?"

"Please, try to understand. You know what all has happened in these past months. I don't want to bother you more. You have already bought so many books for me in this semester."

"Okay, listen. If you don't want to use it, just keep it with you. Swipe it in case of an emergency," he insists.

"Okay!"

"Hey! May I have your number?" Arav suddenly interrupts our talk.

George gives him a harsh look.

“Sorry! Why do you need my number?” I ask him.

“Umm! Just like that!”

“Sorry!”

George and I resume our talk, but Arav keeps looking at us from the cabin inside.

“I’m not feeling good about this guy. Earlier he only used to talk about the class notes and all, but yesterday he just bumped into my practical class and started telling me that he has been trying to talk to me for a long time, but always gets very hesitant. I mean, his way of speaking to me is changing,” I tell George, as Arav moves inside.

“Just ignore him. No need to entertain people like these. In case you still feel uncomfortable, just let me know,” George assures me.

“Listen, mom wanted to meet you today,” he continues to say.

“Oh! Really? When?”

“Today, in the morning.”

“So, when are you taking me home?”

“Let’s go now.”

“Sure!”

As I reach his place, his mom hugs me as if I am her own daughter and gets me a glass of juice.

“I have been asking this boy to bring you home. Actually, I was cleaning the cupboard in the next room and I found quite a few books related to software development and programming concepts. So I thought maybe you’d be interested in taking some of them home.”

"Oh! Sure, maa. I would love to. In fact, I was really looking out to buy some books on programming concepts."

"Come come. I'll show you."

George helps me find some important books for me. It's fun to see him working.

"Maa! I am taking these three books with me." I call his mother maa because she already treats me like her daughter-in-law.

"Sure, baby! You can check if you need anymore."

"Umm! I'll take them again some other time."

"Okay!"

George then drops me near my house.

"Hey! What are you doing?" I ask as he pulls the scarf from my neck and wraps it around him.

"What? I like it."

"Keep it with you then." I wink at him.

As I reach home, my mother bangs the door on my face and dad starts shouting.

"From where did you get these books?" my mother shouts at me.

"I got it from one of my friends from college. Her mother was giving away these books to a library for free, so she asked me to take some."

"A slut, she is. Lets go!" My dad walks out of the house with mom, leaving me completely confused regarding everything that was happening.

"You are gone, sweetheart!" my brother taunts me.

"I don't bother about it anymore. I am already insulted enough," I reply to him.

Let me breathe in the breezes set free,
Let me dance in my own spree.
Life is one and so are the chances which you get,
So grab hold of 'em and leave no traces of regrets.

CHAPTER TWENTY

2nd June, 2014. 10:00 A.M.

With the help of George, I manage to grab a summer internship programme with IBM Gurgaon. As per the guidelines of our college, I needed to get myself engaged in some internship programme to be eligible for additional credits. Today is my first day and George is super excited for me.

My dad asks one of his office workers to drop me at the said location. He doesn't take me along with him for some unknown reason. This guy has come to our house a few times before, but I don't know much about him. As he drives me to my new office on his scooty, I get George's text.

"Reached?"

"I'll call you in some time," I text him back.

After reaching the mentioned address, I immediately dial up George's number.

"Good morning!"

"Good morning, love. So, how did you reach?"

"A guy from my dad's office dropped me here."

"Why didn't your dad go with you?"

"Umm! I don't know. There is something going on in his mind which I am not aware of," I tell him in a low voice.

"Never mind, things will definitely turn around good. Don't worry and all the very best for your first day. Let me know in case you need anything," he wishes me over the call.

"Sure! Love you!"

I get aligned into the IT team with their personnel management project. The day starts with an introduction with the fellow colleagues. Surprisingly, I meet a girl named Ilisa from my college itself. She is a year senior to me. Besides her, there is another girl named Sofi and a guy named Shadab in our team. We are assigned different modules to work on. The whole day, we keep analyzing and reading the given documents, and discuss which language everyone would start the work on. Eventually, I become close friends with the two girls in my team and we three proceed with our respective modules quite efficiently.

Going on tea and coffee breaks, we share lots of stuff with each other. With every passing day, we come to know each other a lot better. Life starts taking a good turn for me as I continue to understand the corporate world outside. George feels very happy seeing me grow all these days. He is very proud of me. Days pass and I become more proficient with my skills and knowledge.

Unfortunately, things don't change much at my house. I have always dreamt of giving my parents all that I can and to show them how much I actually care for them, but

I am unable to make them understand my feelings for them.

They are stubborn on the fact that a girl can't choose her life partner on her own, because she doesn't have this right. No matter how successful she becomes in her career, she needs to abide by the principles of the society she lives in.

I don't understand, where does the society disappear when the girl is insulted by her own in-laws. I see so many cases where the parents forcefully get a girl married to some stranger and then she is beaten up for dowry. Many girls are being assaulted, or are forced to commit suicide, but nobody comes to their rescue at that time.

For which society should a girl think then?

Her whole life, she needs to follow the orders given by her parents and then she is not even allowed to choose the right life partner for herself.

I have grown up seeing my own parents quarrelling with each other. There has not been a single day when I see them sitting with each other and sharing their feelings, their emotions, their love for each other.

I hate this custom where you don't let a girl talk to strangers, but ask her to sleep with one. Whenever my mom takes me out to the market or to some relatives' house, I am not allowed to talk the way I do.

Why should I match the tone of my speaking with my uncle's daughter?

She talks in her own tone and I talk in mine. Why should I run after a government job just because my cousin is doing it?

Why am I always compared to others, when I am unique myself?

Why should I follow the society and its meaningless policies?

When a girl gets married to a person of a different caste, she is disowned by her family, and when the girl is molested for dowry, even then she is disowned. She is then asked to make her own way and to adjust.

Why can't we understand that before belonging to any society, we belong to humanity?

Humans are known for their feelings of love, compassion, gratitude and kindness. No other animal on earth possesses these attributes. By binding girls in this hypothetical cage of the society, we are just snatching away their fundamental rights to live the way they want.

I don't know when my parents would understand this thing and when they would set me free to make my own choices.

Many times, all you can ask yourself,

Is to be strong.

Saying this won't solve the problem,

But will make you gather the courage to endure the tough times.

CHAPTER TWENTY ONE

21st June, 2014. 07:00 P.M.

Like every day, I come back home from my extra classes at NIIT Gurgaon. On my way back home, I meet up with George again to pick up some more spare books from his place. With two fat books in my hand, I start walking upstairs to my room. My mom opens the door and throws the books from my hands. She suddenly starts criticizing me again. Dad, on the other hand, simply stands behind mom and gives me a grim look.

"Where were you?" my mom lashes at me.

"I was at the institute. What happened?" I know something terrible is about to come my way.

"Your dad was standing near the bus stop and he didn't see you coming from the same way. Tell me, where were you?" Mom starts yelling at me.

Dad grabs hold of me tight by my upper arm and drags me to the bedroom, where I fall on the floor. He takes his belt out and starts beating me, without even noticing where I am being hit. He keeps abusing me the whole time, while my mom stands beside him and watches me cry.

He continues to ask me where I was and I keep saying the same thing. After continuously slaying me with that leather belt, he asks, “Where is it?”

“What?”

“The card.”

“Which card?”

He hits the belt on my face.

“You motherfucker! Where is that bloody debit card?”

“I don’t have any card,” I lie.

“You don’t know where it is?” He comes near me, holds my hair tightly and bangs my head against the wall.

I don’t utter a word. He keeps beating me like his slave and I continue getting beaten up. After all, he is my dad.

He grabs my t-shirt, pulls me towards him forcefully and then throws me back. Again, he pulls me towards him and then throws me away again.

My body has turned into stone now. No matter how many times he hurls me on the floor, I don’t feel it anymore.

“Get that card now!” He kicks me on my stomach.

I crawl to my room and hide the card in my waist belt. My mom comes after me quietly, trying to peep in and see where I had hid the card.

“You better get that card, or be ready to see more. BITCH!” My mom pinches me on my right arm.

I still don't utter a word. I go back to dad and tell him that there is no debit card with me.

For one complete hour I am beaten, slapped, criticized for being a girl and insulted for having fallen in love.

"You whore! You are not my blood. B-I-T-C-H. Tell me, how many boys have you slept with? Tell me." He turns violent and gives me another kick in my abdomen.

My mom, on the other hand, just looks at me with a disgusted look, as if I am not her daughter and keeps poking dad the same way she generally does.

Then I hear my dad saying something to my mom.

"You know what, I touched her body last night when she was half-asleep to know what a slut she is…"

I can't believe my ears.

Today, I was telling George how I had felt someone's hand on my chest last night. I was sleeping and when I became conscious, there was no one but only dad sleeping behind me. I then reminded myself that it might be a dream. How could one touch me like that when dad's right behind me, and I went back to sleep again.

Dad continues to tell mom about how he touched me and mom just keeps abusing me.

"How could he? How dare he? Is he my father, or am I actually not his daughter?" I start asking myself. I feel disgusted with my body.

"Are these my parents? Do parents do this to their child? I can't believe this. Where am I? Who are these people?" I keep murmuring to myself, turning completely mad.

My mom, instead of questioning dad about what he did, decides to take me to a doctor to find out about my virginity.

I feel shameful. I feel disgusted.

Yes, this is the society we live in. This is where I am born. My mind stops thinking. I want to erase every memory from my mind which says that these people are my parents. I don't want them to be called as my parents. It's midnight already and they haven't yet stopped.

Since this isn't enough for them, my mom goes to my study room, takes out my school mark-sheets, scholarship letters and certificates, and starts burning them. Dad, on the other hand, starts tearing my college books, telling me that I don't deserve education.

Seeing them do all this, I promise myself that no matter what happens, I'll stand for my love. My parents' views don't matter to me now, and how they treat me is their choice.

George and I love each other and God knows how pure this love is. My parents keep shouting and screaming, but their voices do not reach me anymore.

After all this drama, they go back to their bedroom and sleep, but I remain standing there in my room the entire night.

At around 3:00 A.M., I dial up George.

"Hey, wifey. What happened? All good?" he asks, turning completely blank.

"George, if I come to you right now, at this point of time, carrying nothing with me but only lots and lots of love for you, will you accept me?"

"Yes!" he answers back, without giving it a second thought. "Did something happen at your place again?" he continues to ask.

After a long silence, I break down in front of him and tell him all that I am going through. My hands start shivering and my voice gets fainter.

"How could they?" George gets out of his bed and tells me that he is coming.

"Okay! I'll wait for you," I agree.

"I have earned these certificates by my hard work and knowledge, and I won't let anyone destroy them," I say to myself while keeping my half burnt certificates and remaining mark-sheets in my bag.

After half an hour, George calls me back.

"Sarah! Listen carefully."

"George! Are you here? Should I come downstairs?" I ask him, turning completely breathless.

"Sarah! Wait a minute. Listen to me carefully."

I calm myself down and listen to George.

"Look, if we elope now, your parents will file a complaint against us and may charge both of us with false allegations. As of now, you are their legal daughter and I can take you away with me only after we get married in the court-of-law and you become my legal wife. I love you a lot, Sarah, and I promise to take you out of this hell as soon as I can."

"George, I love you. Can't we get married right now?"

"We can, but I'll need to talk to a lawyer first and no courts will be open tomorrow. If we take a hasty decision right now, your parents may take a legal action against us or put a false allegation that I took you away with me forcefully and tried to do you wrong. I have talked to my mom about everything. We are all with you, Sarah. Don't worry. Within a few days, I'll take you out of this hell. I am sorry, you are going through all of this because of me."

"No, George, this is my decision. I love you and I have no shame in accepting it. I'll wait for your message. Please take me out of this filth," I say to him while crying.

"Don't cry, my love. Trust me, I won't let you go through this for long. Go wash you face and believe in what I've said," George tries to calm me down.

I go and wash my face. Looking at myself in the mirror, all I can see is swollen eyes, bruises on my neck and cheek, messed up hair and somewhere, a ripped soul.

If, by chance, you get in a dilemma,

If, by chance, you get depressed 'cause of your inner conflict,

If, by chance, you need to decide between the right and wrong,

Listen to only one person,

And that's you!

CHAPTER TWENTY TWO

22nd June, 2014. 06:00 A.M.

I couldn't sleep the whole night. I sit on the chair in my study room, and try to remove the stains of the dark kajal pencil, which my dad had drawn all over my books. As the clock strikes 6:00 A.M., I pull on my trouser and a shirt, carry my bag in which I had kept all my certificates and walk out of the house, as if I don't plan on coming back.

I walk through the abandoned streets of the city with a single thought on my mind - to meet George.

As I keep walking on the road, an auto driver comes my way. I sit in the auto and direct him to George's house. As I reach his house, I ring his door bell and his uncle opens the gate. I rush inside and start looking for George. I move to his bedroom and there he is, lying on the bed, looking at the ceiling with the phone kept beside him.

"George!" I rush towards him and hug him as tight as I can.

He presses me close to his heart.

When he sees my scars, a tear drop trickles down his cheeks. It makes me cry as he moves his fingers over my face to feel the pain.

"Don't cry, Sarah. Don't. You are with me now. I won't let anything happen to you now. Shhh! That's it. You have had enough now. Just calm down. Hold my hand."

He hides me between his wide shoulders and slips his hand into mine, holding it the same way he had done that night on that isolated street, when he promised to always be with me.

We get lost in each other. I can feel our hearts beating as one.

"Sarah?" George's mom sees me.

She gets me a glass of water as I get hiccups while crying. She calms me down and makes me sit with her. After listening to the entire thing, she hugs me tightly and then makes a warm cup of tea for me.

"Maa! I can't let this happen to Sarah," George says to his mom, affirming that we want to get married as soon as possible.

It's been hardly 20 minutes, when the door-bell rings. I have a very strong feeling that it's my parents. My brother might have guided them on the way to George's house.

"Please hide me, George, or they'll kill me. I don't want to see them again." I hold George's hand with both my hands and hide my face in his shirt.

He takes me to another room near the dining and asks me to wait there till he talks to my parents along with his mom.

I can't see what's happening outside as I have locked the room from the inside. However, I can listen to the talks.

"Where is Sarah?" my mother asks George's mom.

"She is here, with us."

"I want to meet her."

"Please sit with me. Sarah is scared, she is in another room. I'll call her. But before that, I want to ask you, why do you treat this girl in such a manner. She kept crying when I saw her this morning. She has so many marks on her face and neck. We should not treat our kids this way," George's mom confronts my parents.

"See, Sarah is our daughter and we can treat her the way we want. No one can tell us what is to be done and what not. That's our personal matter," my father replies.

"A father is not allowed to touch her daughter the way you did."

"I am her father and I'll do whatever I want."

"Then there are many women cells which will help teach you what is right and what not," George's mom continues to say.

George then asks me to open the door and come out.

"Please…I don't want to see them. Please let me stay here." I request George.

"Sarah! I am with you. Don't worry, I won't let anything happen to you," George holds me by his right hand, while his left hand rests on my shoulder and we both go in front of my parents.

My mom starts crying loudly, criticizing me on how I have insulted them.

"This girl, she has insulted us in front of the whole world. I don't know who taught her these dirty things like love and all. What did we not do for her? But, she…she is a disgust to our family. Look at her dad, he is so ashamed of her."

"And Sarah?" George's mom leans closer to my mother.

"What about Sarah? Have you ever talked to Sarah about what she has inside her? Have you ever taken the time out to talk to her about what she wants to do in her life? When your husband was doing all those creepy things with your daughter, why didn't you stop him? As a woman, do you think it was right?"

"She has insulted us…" my mom continues to say. "Our society doesn't accept love marriages. It's a shame for us and I won't let this girl destroy the respect that we have in our society. Her father would rather kill her than to let her get into all this."

"You cannot do this to your kid. This is not the right way…" George's mom tries to explain to my mother.

"Please…don't teach me." My mother looks at me with a grimace. She then holds my hand tightly and pulls me towards her.

"Please don't do this to her. You should at least talk to her as a mother."

"You love George?" my mother asks angrily. "ANSWER ME?"

"YES! I LOVE GEORGE…" I answer her back in the same tone.

She leaves my hand forcefully and starts staring at George. He comes closer to me and sits beside me.

"You want to get married to him?"

"YES!" I confess proudly in front of my parents.

My father gets up and walks over to George and says, "Keep her as long as you want to enjoy her. When you are done, let me know."

George closes his fist in anger as my dad walk out of the room.

"You are not my blood…" he says.

"Listen, both of them are adults and they can take their own decisions. We should not treat them like this…" George's mom tries to explain to my mother.

While all this is happening, George secretly hands me a piece of paper. I fold it and hide it in my fist.

The papers reads, *JUST TWO DAYS.*

I look at George and blink my eyes in a yes.

My mother makes me get up and drags me out of the room, instructing me to go home with them.

"Maa! Please stop them. I'll stay here. George, please let me stay here. Please! They'll kill me."

"Just wait for two more days, Sarah." George holds my hand and promises me that he'll not let me endure all this for more than two days and that I should wait for him.

"Go with your brother." My mother pushes me towards the main gate.

I sit on the back seat of the scooty and my brother drives me to our house. While sitting there, I remind myself to just be strong.

"I have dealt with so many things till now. It's just a matter of two more days and then, George will take me out of this shit. No matter how much I'm beaten or abused, I'll bear it all for George."

I say it to myself.

On the way to our house, the scooty gets knocked down by a car and we both get thrown off to one side of the road. My brother starts bleeding as he lands face-first on the concrete put aside on the road, while I get a slight jerk in my knee.

My mother had taken away my phone from me the previous night and my brother had left his phone at home too. I request the guy whose car had banged into the scooty to dial a number.

"Hello, George…George??" My breath gets hitched.

"Sarah? What happened?"

"Our scooty got knocked down by a car and Dhruv is bleeding."

"What? Wait, I am coming." George rushes from his house and reach the spot in a couple of minutes. He then takes Dhruv to a nearby hospital hurriedly and enquires if I have gotten hurt as well.

"You are a curse to the family. Look what you have done to your brother." My mother keeps crying and abusing me all the way.

"Dhruv was riding the scooty at high speed. What's my fault in that? He is still only 15 years old. Why do you allow him to ride that thing?"

"Now you have got the guts to argue with me? GO HOME. I AM COMING WITH YOUR FATHER. You won't understand this way. I'll teach you how to behave." She asks me to go home and calls my father to inform him about the incident.

The scars of your face,

The bruises on your neck,

Will eventually be your source of strength and wisdom.

CHAPTER TWENTY THREE

22nd June, 2014. 09:00 P.M.

"Hello. George?"

"Sarah? You got your phone back?"

"No! I begged Dhruv to lend me his phone for a few minutes."

"Did your parents say anything to you again after returning from the hospital?"

I stay quite.

"Sarah? Are you there?" George asks again.

"Yes. They did."

"WHAT?? I talked to them at the hospital and requested them to not treat you like that again."

"Dad threw my books away and placed his shoes on my study table. He started beating me again. Mom was talking to my grandma and told her that they'll take me to her place soon and would get me married to some guy there…" I tell George.

"Don't worry. I'll talk to the lawyer tomorrow. Till then, just stay calm and remember that I am always with you. Also, please do reach your internship office the day after tomorrow. Do anything, but please don't miss your office on Wednesday."

"Okay!"

"Love you, my wifey! Now smile…the way you do when you see me."

"Hmm, I love you, George."

I disconnect the call and quickly hand the phone over to Dhruv, as I hear my mother coming.

"What are you doing here?" she asks me.

I stare back at her without saying a word, as I have grown tired of answering the same things again and again.

"Can't you hear what I just asked you?" she shouts. "Come, your dad is calling you."

I stand up and make my way to his room with short steps, wondering what else would happen now.

"So, what do you want me to do with you?" My father asks me while spinning his mobile phone between his fingers. "Give me your phone." He starts going through all my texts, call logs and photos in the phone.

"Where else have you been with that guy? I know, you both have been outside this city as well. Tell me where else have you been?"

"I haven't," I reply in a faint tone.

"Come again?"

"I haven't."

"You think I'm a fool?" He starts laughing.

"Do you know, I chopped off your aunt's head when I saw the love letter her boyfriend gave her. You can now imagine what I can do with you."

I stay quiet and listen to every word of his, telling myself only one thing - *only two days*.

He grasps me by my neck and says, "If you had told me this earlier, I would have satisfied your lust…"

I close my eyes in shame.

He then throws me back, still abusing and criticizing me.

My mother stands beside me, listening to all the shit but doing nothing. I remember the day when I saved up fifty rupees to buy her a set of earrings for her birthday. How happy she was then! Now, when every piece of me is being put to shame, she just stands there like a statue, as if I never belonged to her.

Suddenly, everything starts blacking out in front of me and I collapse on the floor. My head had struck the armrest of a wooden chair near me.

After around half an hour, when I open my eyes, I find myself in the same position - collapsed, with that heavy wooden chair lying over my back.

I get up and feel myself very week, as I haven't eaten anything since the previous night. Neither has George, I believe.

Going to my room, I lie down on the floor, join my hands with my head bent down and pray, "Dear God! If my love is true for George and so is his, please get us tied together forever."

I'm thankful for all that you have given to me,
The pain, the torture, the insult.
'Cause all this has made me realise my endurance capabilities.

CHAPTER TWENTY FOUR

23rd June, 2014. 11:00 A.M.

"Wear this from today onwards and forget that you are ever going to study again."

My mom hands me a torn down t-shirt and asks me to do the dishes and the laundry.

Once I finish off with these chores, I am called to the dining area.

While reading the morning newspaper, mom says, "You have to come along with us to the police station."

My eyes turn up and I look straight into her eyes.

"We are filing a legal charge against George, that he has been stalking you for the last few months and that he has molested you on your way to college too," she continues.

"Don't think of running away again, or I won't leave you capable of doing that anymore. You didn't answer to what I said."

I nod my head in affirmation and then I am asked to leave.

My father talks to someone over the phone and tells him about George. He then asks him to get the paper work ready to get George charged with the false allegation and also confirms that he'll be visiting the police station on Wednesday for the same. After this, I come to know that the person he was speaking to was a police officer himself.

In the evening at around 4:00 PM, my parents lock me up at the house and go out.

Fortunately, I find a phone lying under the pillow. My brother generally keeps his phone under his pillow after playing games online.

I hurriedly dial up George and inform him about the entire thing.

"Don't worry! The police is not so stupid," George says.

He makes me talk to his mom, as I get depressed.

"Beta! Don't worry."

"But Maa, my parents were discussing taking me to the police station and file a false case against George. I won't do it."

"Just stay calm. Things will fall into place soon. Take care of yourself."

I had never thought that my parents could go to this extent. They have crossed their limits. I am a captive in my own house and am treated worse than an animal.

Looking at myself in this condition, I feel the harsh reality of the society we live in.

There are so many girls out there in the world who face the same thing that I am facing, but not everyone has the strength to fight against it. Their screams die with them in the suffocating society they live in. In a democratic country like this, for how long will a woman keep paying for her choices, her dreams and her desires? If she is not safe within her own family, how will she be able to survive in the world outside.

Whether it is the corporate sector, the entertainment industry, or the media industry, many will stand up to exploit her. This lust in everyone's eye is never ending. It's not that only women face this insult, men do too. Even kids become the victim of this assault.

Do people like these belong to the human race?

Why should we, as women, be ashamed of being who we are. Why should we be instructed on what to do and what not to do? Who has given this right to the so-called society?

If one flips through the pages of the newspaper, one can view innumerable cases like that everyday. I feel shattered when I read of an eight month old girl who has just come out of her mother's womb and is ripped just to satisfy a man's lust. It's difficult to understand this psychology.

It's heart wrenching.

A person can be locked in a room for days,

But not her conscience.

You can trap the materialistic,

But not the spiritual.

CHAPTER TWENTY FIVE

24th June, 2014. 06:00 P.M.

"We'll reach there by Wednesday. Yeah! Don't worry, we are not allowing her to go anywhere. I don't know where I failed in my upbringing." I hear my mother talking to my grandma over call.

She keeps cursing me for being her daughter, as if it was my choice to be so.

Listening to her gossip, I look at the wall clock and wonder when all this torture would end.

After a couple of minutes, dad comes into the room, stares at me and pushes some dal and chapati in front of me.

"EAT IT!" Mom yells at me while still on the call.

"I don't want to," I refuse.

It has been two days since I've eaten anything, but I don't feel hunger anymore. The only feeling I crave for now is that of freedom, freedom from this captivity.

After constant refusal, my dad opens my mouth forcefully and stuffs food inside till I vomit everything out and almost collapse to the ground. Even my body knows that my soul is yearning for George and not for food.

Following this, at around 9:00 PM, mom makes me wear the same pair of jeans and shirt that I had worn two days ago and asks me to come along with her.

Back in my mind, I feel worried if she is taking me to the cops.

Surprisingly however, she takes me to her friend's place.

"Why, beta? What are you doing with your life? Who's this guy George? Forget about him. I'll get you married to the son of a reputed IAS personnel. Trust me, you'll have a lavish life. Do what your parents say."

Her friend tries to brainwash me. At this point, whosoever is coming to me is just telling me what I'm supposed to do, rather than asking me what my heart wishes for.

My mom's friend keeps trying to convince me and I just listen to her with my head resting on my palms. After two long hours of getting anti-love lessons from her, my mom finally takes me back home.

While everybody else sleeps in their rooms, I stay awake in my study, staring at the walls and the posters with motivational quotes that I had stuck on them.

"This is my last night with you all." I place my hand on my study table and the other stuff in my room, trying to feel them, as if they have got life in them and can hear me.

"You've all been there with me for quite a long time, but now it's time to say goodbye. We might never meet again." I sit on my chair and rest my head down over my books scattered on the table.

My eyes roll up to see every single thing present in the room, making me completely nostalgic.

From that handmade pen stand to my last college assignment, everything catches my sight like never before.

Thinking about what George might be doing right now, I dial him up from my brother's phone that I had slipped away from him.

"Hey!" I whisper.

"Sarah! You haven't sleep yet? It's 3:00 AM."

"I know. Why didn't you?"

"Just finalizing the blueprint for tomorrow."

"Blueprint?"

"Ya! The blueprint to elope with you…"

"How do you manage to lighten my mood even in a serious situation like this?"

"Anything for your happiness…"

I smile.

"Are you coming to office tomorrow?" George asks.

"Yes, I will."

"Have your parents agreed to it?"

"No, I haven't even spoke to them about this. They are more occupied with planning to take me to the police station tomorrow."

"Then how will you come?"

"I don't know, but I believe that things will turn around on their own to tie us together forever…"

"See you tomorrow then!" George smiles and blows me a kiss over the call.

Love never binds,

It liberates…

CHAPTER TWENTY SIX

25th June, 2014. 07:30 A.M.

I stayed awake the whole night, thinking about how I would move out of the house today. What would I say to my parents? Would they allow me to go for my internship programme today? When will everything get back into place?

All such questions strike my mind at the same time and make me go into a state of self-questioning. I have no idea how things will take shape on their own, but I only know one thing - a bright new sun is waiting for me, George is waiting for me and all our woven dreams are there waiting for us.

The morning alarm rings and I get up from my chair in the study and walk towards the kitchen for a glass of water. Simultaneously, I start preparing tea for mom and dad.

"So, George's fever is still on your mind?" My mom asks me while taking the first sip of her tea, while dad giving me a nasty grin with his eyes still on the newspaper.

Having no answer for her question, I just stand their in front of them like a culprit, with my eyes looking down towards the floor.

“Can’t you hear me or have you learnt to ignore your parents now?” Mom yells.

“You’ll be happy to know that we are taking you to your grandma’s house and will get you engaged there. Following that, we’ll finalize the date of your marriage. Now you’ll realize your mistake of falling in love and not abiding by our words for the rest of your life.”

I look directly at her, trying to understand their mentality which is making them take such decisions.

“My life is in my hands. I can either lose it following the society and its false customs or I can go for my own choices and lead a life, full of happiness, contentment, self respect and love. Whatever, I have to do, I have to do it now,” my inner voice talks to me.

“And we’ll go to the police station in the evening. So you better be ready for that too,” my dad says.

“Okay,” I nod my head.

“Finally, you’ve learnt to follow your parent’s orders. Good for you.” My mom looks at me with a doubtful face.

“But…” I speak with a faint voice.

“What…?”

“I need to visit my office one last time to submit back the laptop and my office ID card. You can come along if you want,” I finally say it out.

My mom looks at dad and passes him a smile.

"What do you think? Are we stupid? We won't let you walk out of this house," my dad shouts.

"I have told you, you can come along if you want. You can also talk to my colleague Marie and ask her about the office policies," my voice gets more prominent.

Marie and all of my other colleagues know everything about me. She knows George as well, and how we both love each other. I share Marie's number with mom and ask her to dial her up. Without taking much time, my mom makes a call to Marie and asks her about the office culture and policies. She also investigates if George works at the same office.

"George? Who's that, aunty?" Maries questions over the call.

"You don't know him?"

"No."

"Well, this guy has been stalking Sarah for some time now. Does he not work at the same office?"

"No, not at all, aunty. There is no guy named George here. In fact, Sarah hardly talks to anyone here. She just focuses on her daily assignments during her office hours. Sometimes, I accompany her for coffee," Marie tries to convince my mom.

"Oh! Really?"

"Yup."

"Can I ask you for a favor, Marie?"

"Yeah! Please tell me."

“Sarah needs to submit her laptop and ID card at the office. Actually, we are shifting from this place. Can you do this on her behalf?”

“Sorry, aunty, but the employee needs to do that herself. Sarah needs to come here and return all the assets herself. She’ll get her internship letter only after that.”

“Hmm. Okay. Will you please be with her when she comes to the office today? She is not well and might need you assistance.”

“Yeah, for sure.”

“Thanks, dear.”

I take a deep breath of joy.

“Go, get ready. Your father will go along with you.”

“I won’t have this bitch sit in my car. I’ll ask my worker to drop her,” Dad says to Mom.

He calls one of his garage persons and asks him to drop me at the office.

I feel as if I am soon going to fly off from this cage and will smell the fresh air outside. It has been three days since I’ve been captivated, tortured, beaten up, insulted and molested in my own house, but now, it’s my time to fight against all the injustice that has happened with me.

I then put on the same pair of formal trouser and shirt which I had worn to George’s house three days ago. I know I am not going to get back here ever again, I know it very well. There are so many things which I want to carry with me from this place, but unfortunately, I can only take the most precious belongings. I open up my cupboard and take out the ring which tied me to George forever in the eternal bond of love.

With it, I take that every gift of love which George gave me and leave everything else behind.

“Are you ready?” My mom knocks at my door.

“Yeah! Just coming.”

I leave my room with a laptop bag on my back, carrying in it all that I am supposed to take along. I find the guy waiting for me outside. Taking one last glance of the room, I finally step out towards a new beginning.

“Hi, shall we go?” he asks.

“Sure.”

Reaching halfway, I text George.

“George, I am on my way to office.”

“I knew it, my wifey. How are you coming?”

“There is a guy who works for dad. I don’t know much about him. He is dropping me.”

“Cool! As soon as you reach office, just go straight to your work desk and don’t come down till you receive another text from me. I’m reaching there in some time.”

“Okay, I’ll wait for your call.”

“Sarah?”

“Yup?”

“I love you…”

“I love you too, George.”

After reaching the office, I walk straight to my office floor and find myself stuck at the office gate as my ID card doesn’t let me punch in. While beating me, dad had also crushed the ID card, destroying the chip inside it. The receptionist hands me over a temporary card after enquiring about the previous card's condition. I punch in and see Marie waiting for me at my desk. She gives me a tight hug and then takes me to the washroom.

"Sarah, what happened to you? All these marks on your face, what happened?"

I look at myself in the mirror and it takes me few minutes to recognize my face. I tell Marie about everything that I have gone through over the past few days and she bursts into tears.

After about fifteen minutes, I text George.

"George, where are you?"

"*On the road to you*, my wifey."

My heart starts pounding faster and I get goosebumps as my urge to meet George gets more intense with every passing minute. After fifteen more minutes, I receive a call from George.

"Sarah, I am here."

"I am coming downstairs, George. We should leave now, I can't wait more. Please take me away from here…please…"

"I will…"

George checks if the guy who dropped me is still around or not. After ten minutes, he calls me up and asks me to come downstairs. I cover my face with a scarf and reach the entrance gate. A guy then comes up to me and asks me to go along with him. After looking at him carefully, I realize that it's George's friend, Sebastian.

"Where is George?" I ask him as I can't spot his car around.

"He is right there…please come along."

George had parked the car a few feet away from the entrance gate. After walking a few steps, I see him. He looks at me with the same glimmer in his eyes as when he first saw me in that wall like mirrors at the gym. Our eyes grow moist, but we still hold a wide smile on our faces. This feeling can't be explained by mere words, this is something beyond expression. My pace gets faster as I walk towards him, while he almost runs towards me. I hide myself in his wide arms that wrap tightly around me.

"Sarah…you have had enough now. I won't let anyone come close to you from this moment on." He holds my face in his palms and kisses me on my forehead. We then get inside his car and his other friends follow us in.

George has already planned everything. Within half an hour, we reach one of Delhi's most renowned temples. All the required arrangements had already been taken care of. There are fresh flowers decorated all over the place and all the ingredients required to complete the wedding rituals are already there.

"George…my mom's calling." I tell him, getting nervous.

"Don't worry…"

I nod my head and keep the phone back in my bag, putting it on silent mode.

With our fingers tangled with each other's, we walk towards the pious place where we would get tied to each other forever. As we walk, I look up to George and he looks back at me. We both smile at each other, realizing the feeling of love bloom within us manifold. Following all the wedding rituals, we finally get married to each other in front of God and get tied in the eternal bond of infinite love and care.

Our happiness has no boundaries and our bodies unite as one soul. Love has already healed all our pain.

He slips his hand to my waist and I let my fingers run through his hair. As my gaze rests on his face, his warm breath rushes over my face and our lips get locked. He kisses away every tear that flows down my cheeks.

"You are my life, Sarah…and I love you…"

"And you are mine…..I love you so much, George…"

We get lost in each other.

We are then asked to sign a marriage certificate as the legal proof of our marriage. On our way back home, I file an FIR against my father for having molested and physically tortured me. Following this, he is called and informed about everything.

George's mother and the rest of his family welcome me with open arms and unconditional love.

It's our love because of which I am alive today.

George has kept all the promises that he made to me and I promised to always be with him too. Our love for each other has taught me how pious and beautiful this feeling is.

Love doesn't search for fair bodies, but for pure souls!

This story is based on author's real life!

Author's Bio

Shally Gulshan Sharma is an Indian author who writes fiction. She was born on the 10th of March, 1994, in the state of Madhya Pradesh (Ujjain) in India. She successfully completed her graduation in Computer Science and Engineering from Amity University, Haryana in 2016. She secured first division and had stood as an academic achiever and scholarship holder throughout her academic performance.

Besides this, she has published four research papers in New York's International Journal of Computer Applications on topics mainly concerning machine learning and seam carving techniques, in the year 2015.

While in college, she was actively involved in cultural activities and also holds a gold medal in poetry writing. She is a perfect mix of all flavours of life.

At present, she lives in Gurgaon, Haryana and is pursuing a career as an IT-Manager at a renowned MNC. She likes to travel to unexplored places and spend time with her loved ones. She believes that life's true wealth is love and if it happens to you, you've conquered the universe.

For updates from her and to know more about her, follow her:

On Facebook: www.facebook.com/SheliGulshan.27
On Instagram: shallygulshan
On Yahoo: shallygulshan.sharma@yahoo.com
On Gmail: shallygulshan@gmail.com

Gulshan Shally